Hooray!
It's
a Duck Day!

Jennifer Maze Brown

Illustrated by Sally Schaedler

CPH
SAINT LOUIS

For Sarah, Jonathan, Rebekah, and Suzanne,
who taught me about duck days to begin with
and helped me find the words

In appreciation of our own Nana (and Papaw),
who joyfully remind us daily that
God makes no mistakes

With gratitude to Marlene Bagnull,
who helped me find and enter God's open door

To Donnie, who always knew

1 2 3 4 5 6 7 8 9 10   07 06 05 04 03 02 01 00 99 98

Emily woke early in her grandmother's soft bed. Raindrops drummed *rat-a-tat-tat* on the window.

She rubbed sleepy eyes and peered outside. "Oh, no!" she wailed. "Nana, it's raining! What about our picnic?"

"Hooray! It's a duck day!" Nana laughed, peeking in the room. "Dry your eyes, honey. God makes no mistakes.

"A duck day is as much fun as a dozen picnics. Come on, you'll see!" encouraged her grandmother.

"There's a surprise for breakfast!" Nana announced. "Duck day doughnuts, oatmeal with chocolate chips, and orange juice with floating frozen fruit! Yes, ma'am, duck days are God's good gift, and they are loads of fun."

Emily eagerly sipped the sweet juice and chewed a chocolate chip. She spun a doughnut on her little finger, nibbling around it like a tiny mouse. "This is great, Nana! But it's still raining. We can't have our picnic."

"Sometimes God gives us rain when we had planned on sunshine," explained Nana. "But don't worry. He always does what is best for us. He packs even rainy days full of good things. Shall we go looking for them?"

Emily grinned and grabbed her grandmother's hand. "Sure, let's go," she said.

"Let's sing silly songs and prance on pretend ponies. Let's dance until we are dizzy in fancy old frocks," Nana said.

Emily and Nana sang and pranced and danced and finally fell in a giggling heap on the floor. "Aren't duck days fun?" asked Nana.

"Duck day dancing is super fun!" laughed Emily. "But it's still raining. Maybe we'd better keep looking."

"Good idea," Nana grinned. "Let's go look for more!"

"We can color cute kitty cats! Draw daffy dogs! Paint pretty posies! Cut curlicues! Aren't duck days fun?" Nana asked.

Emily lazily uncurled a curlicue and added a splash of bright pink to her posy. "Painting is almost as much fun as a picnic," she said slowly, "but it's still raining. Let's keep looking."

"It's tea party time," said Nana. "Tiny tea cups and tiny tea cakes. Aren't duck days fun?" The rain danced pitter pat on the roof and pelted the window near the tea table.

Emily looked over her tiny tea cup at her grandmother. "Duck days *are* fun, but I still wish we could have picnicked outside," she answered wistfully.

"Outside," chortled Nana. "Duck days are even more fun outside. Come on, let's go see!"

"We'll walk in whispery wetness—
underbrella!" Nana caught a raindrop on her
tongue. "Tiddly pink! Tastes pink!"

Emily giggled and caught a raindrop on her
tongue too.

"Come on," said Nana. "Let's pounce puddles! Pit pat puddle SPLAT!"

"Hey, I can do that, too!" Emily's boots landed SPLASH in a great big puddle.

"Aren't duck days fun even if we can't have a picnic?" asked Nana as she laughed. Emily just flashed her wonderfully wet smile and pounced two more puddles.

Back inside, Emily's grandmother sliced two rosy apples, and they sat by the window to share them. As they munched the crunchy sweet slices, Nana suddenly cried, "Oh Emily, look!"

"A rainbow!" Emily squealed, running to the window. "I *love* rainbows!"

"So do I," replied Nana thoughtfully. "You know, it takes a duck day to have a rainbow. They don't come on days without rain. And every time God sends a rainbow, He reminds us that He keeps His promises."

"What kind of promises?" asked Emily.

"Well, God makes lots of promises," answered Nana, "but His best promise of all was to send Jesus to be our Savior."

They quietly watched until the rainbow faded to only a thread of faint color across the gray sky.

"Now," said Nana. "Let's snuggle under my cozy quilt and hear a hundred happy books."

Emily crawled into Nana's lap in her old rocking chair and they read and rocked, nodded, and napped.

Emily's grandmother softly sang,

> *I love you bright as the rainbow,*
> *I love you as deep as the sea.*
> *I love you as tall as a mountain,*
> *And I'm so glad God gave you to me!*

Emily gently traced the lines on Nana's face with her finger. "Nana, you were wrong," she said seriously, but with a twinkle in her eye. "Duck days are *not* as much fun as a dozen picnics."

"What?" asked her grandmother, so startled that she stopped rocking.

Emily giggled and grinned. "They're more fun than a *hundred* picnics!"

Nana hugged Emily close and smiled. "Yes, honey. Duck days are God's good gift. And God makes no mistakes."